Where's Gomer?

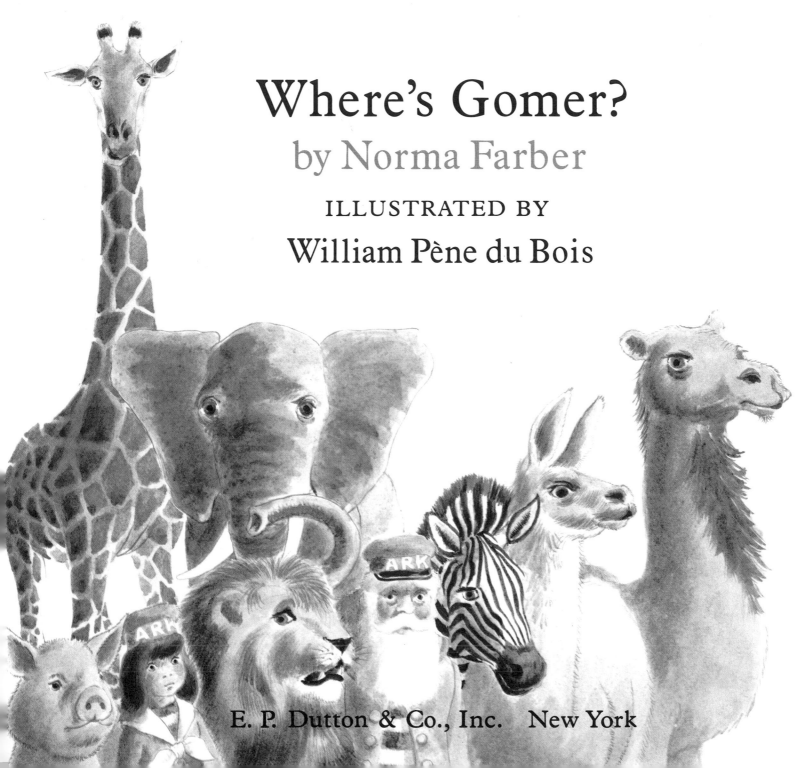

Where's Gomer?

by Norma Farber

ILLUSTRATED BY

William Pène du Bois

E. P. Dutton & Co., Inc.   New York

For Steve,

who almost never misses the boat

Text copyright © 1974 by Norma Farber
Illustrations copyright © 1974 by William Pène du Bois

Library of Congress Cataloging in Publication Data

Farber, Norma   Where's Gomer?

SUMMARY: The voyage aboard the Ark begins sadly since
Noah has been forced to sail without his favorite grandson.

[1. Stories in rhyme.   2. Noah's ark—Fiction]
I. Pène du Bois, William, illus.   II. Title.
PZ7.F2228Wh   [E]   74-4039   ISBN 0-525-42590-x

Published simultaneously in Canada by Clarke,
Irwin & Company Limited, Toronto and Vancouver

Designed by Riki Levinson
Printed in the U.S.A.   First Edition
10 9 8 7 6 5 4 3 2 1

Everyone's settled on board the Ark.
We boys are watching the watermark.
It won't be long before we embark.
Where's Gomer?

Noah's enjoying a coffee break.
Grandma, his wife, serves milk and cake,
which we take and take and take and take.
Let's save a few pieces for Gomer's sake.
Where's Gomer?

Japheth and Shem and Ham are here,
sorting the tackle, testing the gear,
for we may be afloat as long as a year.
"We'll manage," says Noah. "Be of good cheer!
Where's Gomer?"

There's Japheth's wife, and Shem's, and Ham's,
shelving the juices, the jellies, the jams,
the bacon, the biscuits, the hickory hams,
answering last-minute telegrams,
unlocking the antelopes from the rams.
     Where's Gomer?

Here's Tubal, here's Magog, and several others:
they're Japheth's sons and Gomer's brothers.
     But where's Gomer?

His cousins are all accounted for:
Asshur, and Aram, and quite a few more.
      But not Gomer.
Has anyone seen him? Scan the shore!

"We saw him climbing a Mackintosh tree,"
cry a pair of field mice. *"Hurry!* piped we,
to the Ark!" "You did?" drawls Noah, slow.
"And when was that?" "An hour ago.
      We saw Gomer."

The father of Gomer peers from the prow.
"Why isn't that rascal on board by now?"
He chews at his beard, he furrows his brow
about Gomer.

The mother of Gomer's in tears. "What a time
to shinny for apples, or just for a climb!
O Gomer!"

With a deep, deep, deep, deep grandfather sigh,
tilting his telescope slightly to spy,
old Noah peers round, while an hour runs by,
and a wind like a paintbrush daubs the sky
the color of tar, or of target's eye....
       Still no Gomer.

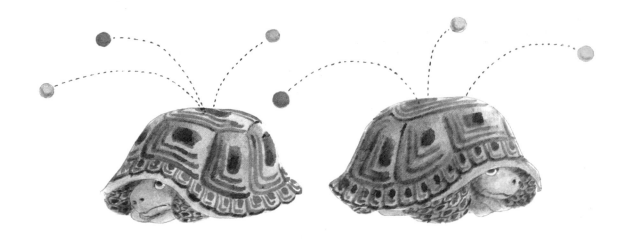

Two turtles rear up with a single voice.
"Mind you, we realize boys will be boys
      like Gomer.

"So we drew in our heads through our safety cracks.
We stood stone-still in our sandy tracks,
as he aimed his marbles onto our backs—
      that Gomer."

That Gomer's mother scatters a sigh
like drops from laundry hung out to dry
in a gale. "O Gomer, O Gomer, O my
      boy Gomer!"

"Then *we* came along. We caught his eye.
He turned to chase us, slithering by.
He couldn't catch up: still, he had to try.
But snakes in the grass can fairly fly
     from Gomer!"

The clouds grow blacker. The bustling crew
leans over the railing for some small clue.
The women are stirring a savory stew
that the tears of a mother have fallen into.
The animals make a loud cry and hue.
"What's to be done? O what shall we do?
The Ark must depart on the striking of two."
     Without Gomer?!

Orders are orders, as Noah well knows.
Commanding his Ark, by the Book he goes.
But without Gomer?!

The cougars recall, and the skunks, and the shrews,
a boy who was fishing a brook—with his shoes.
But that was at noon. No longer it's news
about Gomer.

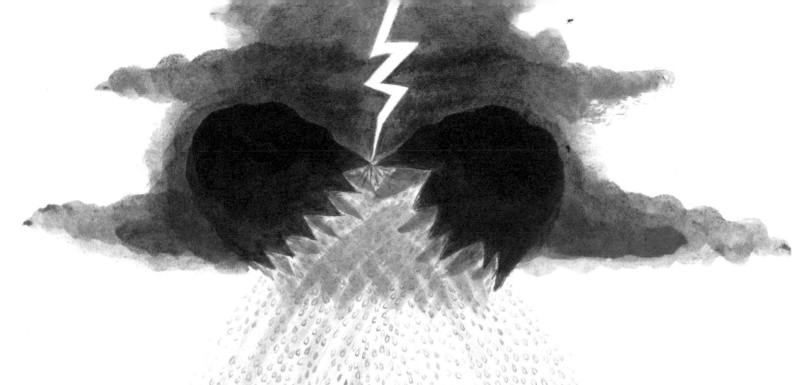

A cloud bursts its buttons. Forth blows a gust.
The Ark—well, the Ark leaves the dock as it must,
minus a boy, and plus great regret—
in the storm and the cold and the waves and the wet—
    yes, for Gomer.

Glum is the voyage. We can't make believe
that it isn't. Deep down in our cabins we grieve
for the fellow we're sorry to leave, yes, leave
    behind: Gomer.

O tempest and flood! O watery ways
of dismal darks and desolate grays!
O deluge! O umpteen nights and days
without Gomer!

O missing nephew, cousin, son!
O grandchild—Noah's favorite one,
named Gomer....

A mountain's looming ahead at last.
The months of sorrow-at-sea are past.
The storm subsides. The waves grow flat.
It seems we ought to rejoice. What *at?*
What's great or glad about Ararat?
What's a miracle—if it comes to that—
        without Gomer?

But rub your eyes, so you see it clear:
Gomer's already arriving here!
A dolphin—whom Gomer's proud to thank—
dumps him dryly up on the bank.
Gomer's the first to disembark.
So he helps us others off the Ark.
      "Hi, Gomer!"

NORMA FARBER is a poet of distinction, a concert singer, and an actress, as well as the author of two picture books, *Did You Know It Was the Narwhale?* and *I Found It in the Yellow Pages*. It wasn't until she became a grandmother that she began to write for children. Her husband, the late Dr. Sidney Farber, was an eminent cancer authority, especially renowned for his care of children. Mrs. Farber, Boston born and bred, received her bachelor's degree from Wellesley College and her master's degree from Radcliffe College. She now lives in Cambridge, Massachusetts.

WILLIAM PÈNE DU BOIS was born in Nutley, New Jersey, but spent most of his childhood in France. Coming from a family background of art and design, he thinks he may have taken "the line of least resistance" when he wrote and illustrated his first book at the age of eighteen. This launched a distinguished career of illustrating his own and other authors' books. In 1948 he received the Newbery Medal for his writing of *The Twenty-One Balloons*. Among his recent titles are *Bear Circus, Call Me Bandicoot,* and *William's Doll* (written by Charlotte Zolotow). Mr. Pène du Bois now lives in Nice, France, in an apartment house practically surrounded by water, which may account for his enthusiasm for *Where's Gomer?*

The display type was set in Plantin and the text type was set in Bookman. The full-color art was prepared in watercolor and the book was printed by offset at Lehigh Press.